The Magic Pear

D1028698

A folk tale from China

Retold by Rosie Dickins

Illustrated by Matt Ward

Reading Consultant: Alison Kelly
Roehampton University

This story is about selfish Shen,

a hungry beggar,

a kind
woman,

some
YUMMY
pears

and a little bit of magic.

3

Shen lived in a little house
with a big garden.

There was a tree in the garden. The tree grew sweet, golden pears.

5

There were too many
pears for Shen. But he
didn't want to share them.

"I'll sell them at the market," he thought.

I'll make lots of money.

So Shen took a box of pears to the market.

A beggar stopped to look.
"Please may I have a
pear?" he said.

"Can you pay?"
asked Shen.

"I don't have any money,"
said the beggar.

"Then go away!"
shouted Shen.

A kind woman
heard Shen shouting.

"Can't you give away *one* pear?" she asked Shen.

"That man is hungry and you have enough to share."

"NO!" shouted Shen.

"Then I'll buy a pear and
give it to him myself,"
said the woman.

16

"Thank you," said the beggar.

That's kind of you.

He ate the pear quickly.

He spat out the seeds.

"Mmm, yummy," he said happily.

"Now, it's my turn to give you a pear."

21

"Aha!" cried Shen. "You DO have money!"

"No," said the beggar.

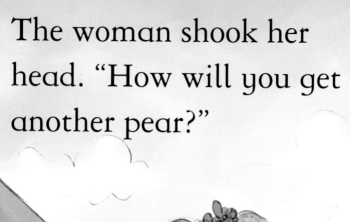

The woman shook her head. "How will you get another pear?"

The beggar smiled.
"I'll show you," he said.

A crowd came to watch.

The beggar dug a hole
and dropped in the seeds.

"May I have some hot water?" he said.

A tea-seller gave him
a teapot.

The beggar poured hot
tea into the hole...

The crowd gasped.
"Look, a shoot!"

It grew into a tree,
with green leaves
and golden pears.

The beggar picked a pear
and gave it to the woman.

34

"Mmm, yummy,"
she said happily.

The beggar turned to the crowd. "Does anyone else want a pear?"

"Me! Me! Me!"
they shouted.

The beggar picked pear
after pear. Soon the tree
was bare.

Everyone got one – even selfish Shen.

Now no one was
watching the beggar.

He chopped down the tree
and strolled away.

Suddenly, Shen looked
around.

All his pears had gone!
And their wooden box
was chopped to pieces.

"It was a trick," he yelled.
"Those pears the beggar
picked – they were mine!"

But the crowd just
laughed.

"Next time, perhaps you'll be less selfish," they said.

The Magic Pear Tree is a traditional tale from China.

Designed by Michelle Lawrence
Cover design by Louise Flutter
Series designer: Russell Punter
Series editor: Lesley Sims

First published in 2009 by Usborne Publishing Ltd., Usborne House, 83-85 Saffron Hill, London EC1N 8RT, England. www.usborne.com Copyright © 2009 Usborne Publishing Ltd.